A GREAT ADVOCATE "KAVIN"

HE IS AN ADVOCATE WHO SACRIFICES HIMSELF .

MUDLIYAR UDAY KUMAR

Disclaimer

This story is little bit different from Tamil language . Because due to the translation issues but book wrote by same author only . Not copied . We were just trying to make the English version of this book so the people can love to read it . This is a short story written by Author Mudliyar Uday Kumar .

A great advocate "Kavin"

Ramu,s family was a rich family. He had two sons. They
were named Kavin and youngest son named Naveen. Kavin
was born in 1970 and Naveen was born in 1976. Ramu was
a police officer in Pune from 1965 to 2005 .
. He died on March 13, 2005 . Now one day Kavin asks his
father, "Can I study for advocate?" His parents said,
"Yes ,you can study for it, but you have to be very quick,
active, and alert." Kavin : Yes my parents .
As he grown up
completed his studies till 12th . He came first

in his school .
So now he choosed the 1ˢᵗ option in his mind.
That first
course, the B.Com course would take 3
years, then 2 years
to complete the LLB. In total ,he took 5 to 6
years to
become an advocate. At the time of studying
for all this,
his age was 25. Few days later the result
came he was pass
in his exams of LLB . He was success and
became a senior
advocate. For 4 to 5 years he received the
simple cases
such as land, injustice and many other
simple cases. Now
one tough case came to Kavin that is the
murder case of
Rana Pratap . K . John was the murderer .
He was the MD
of the Protein Drink Company. . He was the
greedy MD of
the Horlicks company. He used to mix the
some chemicals
which costs less , because of it people who
eats it they like
to eat again and again. His company was
out of India , it
was in Indonesia. He sold the item at double
price and
made more profit. If someone does not buy

the product , he
used to send his rowdy gang to threaten them to buy his
protein products . He was doing everything against the law
due to which so many cases was filed on him . The case
was handed over to Kavin .
So Kavin gathered all the information to prove that he is the
exact murderer . An unknown call came from unknownnumber to him and said, "If you prove that we are the
murderers , then we will kill your father. At that time
K.John came to Mumbai . Kavin did not take it seriously
he told "I am busy in court call me later" .
But Raj did not cut the call and he was trying to threaten
Kavin .
Kavin : If you have that much daring then come infront of
me and deal with me .Now bye,.
K.John worker Raj : Now you will not take it serious, I
know when you will take it serious, just see after coming
from court what happens.
Kavin : I am in Court ,just stop Your foolishness. Will call
you later and talk about this.

Raj : I will deal with you . Don,t talk in
attitude. Bye!
[Now he cut the phone]
Now as he told he killed Kavin's father and
stoll all the
documents from their home.
[1 hours later]
[Kavin,s Mom call him .]
[Kavin attains the call]
Kavin : What happened mom ??
Mom : My son , some of the gang of theives
came to our
house and killed your father and took all the
proof,s which
you have collected.
Kavin : What ? [With shock expression]
Mom I am coming there within 15 minutes .
I am sending
an ambulance please go with father .
Mom : Please come soon.
[Now again Raj calls Kavin]Raj : As I told
you we did it . Go to your home soon
otherwise you can,t be able to save your
father .
Kavin cuts the call……
Now he went to the hospital . He asks to
doctor
Kavin : Doctor what happened to my father
?? , and how he
is now?
Doctor : Sorry we can,t save your father ,
because who have

killed your have used a sharp weapons .
Kavin : Then ?
Doctor : Sorry we are helpless
[Kavin took his father body and did the formalities what
normal people do after death.
Sad days passed .
Now one day
Mother : Kavin ,please get married.
Kavin : No mummy , please .
Mother : If you will not marry anyone then I will not tell
any proof for you in your case .
Kavin: Ok Mom.
[Now after 7 days]
Kavin : Mom can you tell about what they told to you .
Mom : They told that we are from Tigers of Indonesia
gang.
Kavin : And more about them ??
Mom : They told that , we are the workers of K.John .
Kavin : Can you repeat again , I am shooting the video for
proof .
Mom : Ok
[Now Kavin shooted the video and saved it in his mobile .]Now he started to search Rana Pratap,s Company . After
few days he got the address of his company and started to

travel there]
[His company was in Pune]
However he got the address, he went inside the office and
asked to his staffs.
Kavin : Do you know that your M.D Rana Pratap sir died ??
Staffs : Yes sir .
Kavin : Then how the company is running ?
Staffs : Sir before he dies he told that , If anything happens
to me suddenly than Harshal will be the M.D.
Kavin : Who is Harshal?
Staffs : Why you are asking to us sir ?? who are you ??
Kavin : I am an advocate who is handling your boss case .
Staffs : Ok sir .
Kavin : Then tell !
Staffs : Sir Harshal is the P.A of Rana sir .
Kavin : Staffs do your boss has any relatives ??
Staffs : Yes sir he has his relative . He is non other than his
father .
Kavin : Then why he didn,t came here ??
Staffs : Sir he didn,t know only that his son has died . If we
will tell than he can go for sucide .
Kavin : Can you tell me his address ??
Staffs : Sir he live in Gandhi Nagar near

Dany caffe Ratna
apartment .
Kavin : Thank you everyone .
[Before this you have to know this that why
K. John killed
Rana Pratap . Because , before the death of
Rana Pratap 2
days before . K.John went to Rana Pratap to
tell him to buy
the protein drink product which was called
K.J Drink . Hemet Rana Pratap because he
wanted to distribute his
product all over Mumbai . Rana Pratap was
a famous goods
distributor . He use to check one time is it
good for health
or not ? . Now one day K.John and Rana
Pratap met and
they discussed.
K.John : Hi !we met after long time .Is it ??
Rana Pratap : Yes John ,welcome to my
company !tell what
you have to supply . I will supply it in full
India by giving
you 30% profit of it.
K. John : Raj remove that drink powder .
Rana Pratap : Which drink it is ??
K.John : It is a Protein drink .Will you
supply this ??
Rana Pratap : Yes I can .
K.John : Then pass the notice to
Government now .

*Rana Pratap : Wait , first I will do lab
testing of your
product and I will tell you the results ,
because it can also
harmful .
K.John : You have doubt on me ?
Rana Pratap : No I don'tmean that ,But
checking is also
very important , Right ??
K.John : Yes ,yes .
Rana Pratap : Come tomorrow I will tell you
the result .
K.John : Ok bye .
Rana Pratap : Bye
[Now they stayed in a hotel]
One of the worker asked
Raj: John if he find out that the chemical is
mixed in it
then ??
K.John : I will try to convince him .
Raj : If he not accept it and leak that matter
out then ??K.John : Then means ??
Raj : First of all Pune police will catch you
and the second
thing is that they will keep you in their
custody .If this
news will leak over world then ??, Your
company will be
banned
K.John : Before this happens I will kill you
Rana Pratap !.
[Lab test report day*

Rana Pratap : Can I come there to show the
result ??
K.John : Yes you can , Just I am forwarding
the message to
you .
Now Rana Pratap went to John,s given
address
Rana Pratap : Shame on you John
K.John : Why ??
Rana Pratap : Why you mixed chemicals in
it ??
K.John : Don,t tell to anyone please . I will
give you
separate 14 crores to you for that .
Rana Pratap : Now also you are not changed
. You are just
hiding your mistake by money . No ! I will
leak this news
to Government and tell to Government to
bann your
company products in whole world .
K.John : First of all, if you will be alive then
only you can
tell ??
Rana Pratap : What ?
K.John : Raj take his weapon and kill him .
[Raj took that weapon and killed him .]
[This such things was happened before]
[Now come back to present days]
Now after finding the address of Raj Pratap
who is the
father of Rana Pratap he went there and

*reached to his
house . He banged the door .Raj Pratap
opened the door .
Raj Pratap : Who are you sir .
Kavin : Sir I am an advocate .
Raj Pratap : Sir please come inside .
[Kavin sat there and they started having a
short discussion]
Kavin : Sir do you know that your son has
died ??
[Raj Pratap got dizziness and fell down
after listening it .
Now Kavin tried to wake him up . He
Sprinkled bit of water
on his eyes and he was success in waking
him up.]
Kavin : Sir, are you ok ??
Raj Pratap : Yes { by crying }
Kavin : Sir don,t cry ..I am there to resolve
the case . Be
calm .
Raj Pratap : Ok...I was shocked , when I
heard this news as
I didn,t know it because no one informed it
.Even company
staffs also .
Kavin : Sir they was not telling to you
because. If you will
hear it then your bp can become high and
you can be in
difficult sir .
Raj Pratap : Oh ,Ok .*

Kavin : Sir you can tell me that who can kill
your son ? By
your experience .
Raj Pratap : Yes , I think K.John .
Kavin : Sir who is K.John ??
Raj Pratap : He is a very bad & greedy
person who just
fight with my son during school and college
days .
Kavin : More information sir ??
Raj Pratap : I know this much only . You can
ask more
information about them in Pune college .
Kavin : Sir can you tell this all things I will
shoot it and
keep with me .[Now he shooted it and saved
]
Kavin : Thank you sir .
Raj Pratap : I should tell you thank you,
because you are
handling this case very honestly. If K. John
has killed Rana
then give him a diffucult punishment .
K.John also have a
company who adds the chemical in his drink
and he used to
sell in the world .
Kavin : How do you know this sir ??
Raj Pratap : My friend was in England he
told me . His
company was banned in England for this
reason .

Kavin : Thank you so much sir .
And sir , please come on monday in court .
[Now Kavin went to the Pune college .]
He asked and took permission to the
watchman and went
inside.
Mr . Kuldeep : Hi sir
Kavin : Hi , Sir I am a advocate .
Mr. Kuldeep : I know , but why you came
here sir ??
Kavin : Sir can you tell me about K.John and
Rana Pratap
releationship??
Mr. Kuldeep : Oh , K.John is my friend ! . Oh
sorry .
Kavin : Its ok sir .
Mr.Kuldeep : Sir their relationship was not
so good they use
to fight for small things .
Kavin : Sir do you know that Rana has died .
Mr.Kuldeep : No sir !
Kavin : Sir who can kill Rana Pratap tell by
your own
experience .
Mr. Kuldeep : I think 100% that K.John .
Kavin : Sir can you tell all the things which
you just told
now ??Mr. Kuldeep : Yes .
[Now he told all things infront of camera
whatever he told
to Kavin .]
Kavin : Sir from first day ,are you the

principal of this
college ?
Mr. Kuldeep : No sir . My father was there .
But why your
asking it ??
Kavin : Sir you was telling that I am his
friend , thats why .
Mr. Kuldeep : Ok
Kavin : Sir you have K.John ,s Phone number
??
Mr.Kuldeep :Yes see this and note down if
you want then .
[Now Kavin note down the phone number
and told " Sir
come in court on Monday .
Mr. Kuldeep : Ok sir .
Kavin : Sir take my visiting card for any
emergency .
Mr.Kuldeep : Ok sir .
[Kavin went from there]
Now only 2 and a half day is remaining for
case . Kavin
planned one thing that he will call on that
number and trace
him and bring him in the police custody .
Before this
Mr.Kuldeep informed K.John that " he
should be more
attentive from him ." Now what will happen
by reading
book you will understand it .
Kavin called him and spoke to him.

Kavin : Hi !is this K.John ??
K.John : Who are you ??
Kavin : I am Dharmendar and I am product distributor of
India . I have heard about your protein K.J drink .
[Before you all were thinking why Kavin is telling lies
because if he will tell real then K.John will never come to
India . And at that time he was in America ,Florida .]K.John : Then ??
Kavin : Can you bring me 3 lakh sachets of your drink . I
will give you my half share .
[At start he was thinking about this,but because of his
greediness he agreed for it .
Kavin : Ok come to India in Pune to Mini Taj Hotel for
dealing .
[After 1 day passed]
Now K.John came to Kavin .
Kavin talked with him for sometimes and shouted loudly
" Police catch them all".
[Now policemen arrest them all and put him in the jail .
[Now in court]
Kavin : Good Morning your owner .
Chief Justice : Good morning Kavin .
Kavin : Sir today we are here for the case of

Rana Pratap .
Chief Justice :Yes I Know .
Kavin : Sir I want your permission to call
Raj
Pratap .(Father of Rana Pratap)
Chief Justice : Permission Granted . Raj
Pratap ,Raj Pratap ,
Raj Pratap .
[Now Raj Pratap came]
Kavin : Your owner he is the father of Rana
Pratap .
Raj Pratap : Good morning your owner .
Chief Justice : Good morning . What you
think about your
son,s death ??
Raj Pratap : Sir I think that K.John might
have killed my
son .
Chief Justice : How you can tell it ?
[Then he told all things]Advocate Rahul :
Objection your owner.
Chief Justice : Objection disagree
Chief Justice : Kavin you have any more
proof ??
Kavin : Yes your owner . Call Mr.Kuldeep .
Chief Justice: Mr.Kuldeep , M.r Kuldeep, M.r
Kuldeep
Mr. Kuldeep : Good Morning your owner .
Chief Justice : Good morning .
Kavin : Your owner see this video where he
have gave his
proof .

[Chief Justice saw the video and asked .]
Chief Justice : Is this real video and Kuldeep you have told
this in video or anybody .??
Mr. Kuldeep : Your owner,
Chief Justice : What happened??
Mr. Kuldeep : Your owner Kavin forced to tell me like this .
Kavin : No your owner he is telling lies.
Advocate Rahul who was the side of K.John : Your owner
Kavin is wasting the court time . You should put this case to an end .
Kavin : No your owner .
Chief Justice : Silence , Silence ,Silence . Now the result
is . This case has been postponded on Thursday on
afternoon 12.00PM to 1.30 PM . Now everyone can disperse .
Chief Justice : What nonsense Kavin, you have wasted my
time and court,s time also I beleived on you . But instead what you did.
[Now everyone left the court]
Half day passed but no proofs was collected . Kavin was in
tension . Suddenly a phone call came from unknown

number , he picked it up and spokeKavin :
Who is speaking ??
Ramranjan sir : I am Ramranjan the father
of Kuldeep .
Tomorrow I want to meet you to speak
something
important .
Kavin : But sir from first only I am angry on
your son .
Ramranjan sir : Forget that and come
tomorrow in
Hasmukth park .
Kavin : Ok sir .
[In Hasmukth Park in morning]
Kavin: Why did you call me??
Ramranjan sir : You listen and shoot the
video what I am
telling you .
Kavin : Sir I have started the video tell what
you want .
Ramranjan sir : First of all Good Morning
your owner . I
want to tell the truth that my son Kuldeep ,
before coming
to court ,he took 14 crores from K.John at
night as Kavin
went from there and K.John told to tell like
this . I have the
video also see it .
[Then Kavin ended the video]
Ramranjan sir : Give your number I am
sharing this video .

[Then he shared that video and told "I told to you Kavin
that I will be very useful for you in your case.
Kavin : Thank you sir . Because of you this case can come
into end.
Suddenly M.r Kuldeep came there ...
Kuldeep : Father you cheated me know ??
Now John will
kill me .
One Idea if I kill you, then nobody will be there to tell there in the court .
[After telling this he removed his gun and try to shoot his
father but Kavin came in middle the bullet shooted Kavin .
Now Kavin got bleeding from his chest . [Kuldeep cannotrun from there because first only Kavin has put the police security . The police caught him and put him in the jail .
[Now Mr. Ramranjan called Ambulance . Now Ambulance
came and took him to hospital .
Mr.Ramranjan informed
this all thing to his family members . They all came there.
Kavin's Mom and Kavin,s Wife Pooja and his son came .
Now Kavin was took inside the Emergency ward . Doctors

did operation and told to Kavin that he
should rest for 1
month .
Kavin : No doctor in 1 day I have to go to
court , please
help me,do anything please .
Doctor : I will try my best , but you get
stress than it can
lead to your death . For one case you have to
sacrifice
yourself ??
Kavin : Doctor, today I am sacrificing myself
for
tomorrows generations . Mr.Ramranjan
called all who came
on 1st day of case in court . Because Kavin
told him to do
that. .
[1 day passed]
In court
Kavin with slow voice : Good morning your
owner .
Chief Justice : Good morning
Kavin : Your owner see this video and try
understand it .
Now Chief Justice saw that video and
understood it whose
mistake was it . This case came to an end.
Now there is no
way to tell lie so K.John told all the truth
.Result came that
K.John will be put for his death and Kuldeep

will also . As
Kavin heard it he was happy and fell down .
His blood was
flowing again from his body parts . He was
took to hospital
but doctors told " Sorry"we are helpless

All were crying . And the formalities was
done by the
Government, and his body was dig inside the
mud and all
saluted him .
After 20 Years Junior Kavin, Jagdish came
back in the form .
Again one time .
A Great Salute to "Kavin"
By : Mudliyar Uday Kumar .

Contents